Grandfather's Gold Watch

Dedicated to the memory of two great storytellers
Orson and Viola Garff

Thanks to the friends who helped:

Deon Hubbard, Holly H. Daines, Garff Hubbard, Marci H. Groesbeck, Kelly Hubbard, Nina Jorgensen Hubbard, Jennifer Pritchett, Ron Stucki, Harrison and Iva Lou Groutage, Jeri Malouf, Brigham White, Nelson Wadsworth, Steve Murdock, Susan A. Madsen, Peter Garff, Sharon Garff, Jim Jacobs, Ailey Hubbard, Kaye Rhees, David Groesbeck, Peter Daines, Emily, Alex, and Madeline Daines, Jane Broberg, Helen Cannon, Will Pitkins, Julia Barrett, Steve Baker, Joel Lundstrom, Lois Price, Bruce King, Fredrick Nelson, and Christina Nelson.

Library of Congress Cataloging-in-Publication Data
Hubbard, Louise Garff, 1934–
Grandfather's gold watch /written and illustrated by Louise Garff Hubbard.
    p.   cm.
Summary: Peter cherishes the watch his grandfather gives him before his family leaves Denmark for America, and even after losing the watch on the journey to Utah, he remembers its message.
ISBN 1-57345-242-4
[1. Danish Americans—Fiction. 2. Grandfathers—Fiction. 3. Frontier and pioneer life—Fiction.] I. Title.
PZ7.H8587Gr   1997
[E]—dc21   97-2622
                                                                                          CIP
                                                                                          AC

Printed in Mexico
10   9   8   7   6   5   4   3   2   1

Grandfather's Gold Watch

WRITTEN & ILLUSTRATED BY

LOUISE GARFF HUBBARD

SHADOW MOUNTAIN · SALT LAKE CITY, UTAH

Grandfather was working in the garden when Peter arrived. He had not been happy since he learned Peter and his family were planning to leave Denmark and go to America. "I will live and die in Denmark," he had said firmly, "and you should, too." Grandfather had argued with Peter's father and tried to make them stay.

When Peter found Grandfather in the garden, he waited awkwardly for him to speak. Grandfather went right on hoeing the flowers, so Peter spoke first. "Grandfather, tomorrow I'm leaving for America," he said. "I've come to tell you good-bye."

At last Grandfather stood up and looked at Peter sternly. His bushy eyebrows were pulled together in a frown. But finally he sighed and set down his hoe. Together he and Peter walked to a bench under the shaded arbor in the garden.

"How old are you, Peter?" Grandfather asked.

"Twelve," he replied. "Well, not quite. I'll be twelve next week—when I'm sailing on the ship to America."

"Peter, you are my eldest grandson." Grandfather spoke slowly and sadly. "America is far away, and I am old. I will probably never see you again after you leave Denmark. I have something to send with you. Not your birthday present, but two gifts from me. Your first gift is my name. I gave it when you were born and christened Peter Nels Jorgensen. It is an honorable name in Denmark. Take our name to America and make it honorable there, too." Grandfather was very solemn, but his face softened. "And now the second gift."

Grandfather undid the gold watch from his vest. As long as Peter could remember, his grandfather had worn the handsome timepiece with the gold chain dangling across his middle. Grandfather opened the watchcase and let Peter read the inscription—the name they shared. He took Peter's hand, put the watch into his palm, and folded the young, thin fingers over the treasure with his own rough, worn fingers.

"My timepiece and my name belong to you now," Grandfather said kindly. "I cannot ask you every year on your birthday how you have treated these gifts. You must ask yourself for me,

What have I done with my name?

What have I done with my time?

With great surprise and respect, Peter took the gold watch. Grandfather had always been very proud of the watch, and Peter knew it was hard for him to give it away. "Thank you, Grandfather," he said softly. "This will always remind me of you and Denmark."

The next morning Peter and his family left Copenhagen on a sailing ship headed for America. Sailing over the ocean wasn't as exciting as Peter thought it would be, and to make matters worse, he was very seasick. Sometimes the watch helped him forget his misery. It was smooth and cool and comforting. He often held it to his ear and listened to the ticking sound and thought about Grandfather's words.

One day the captain of the ship stopped Peter on deck to admire the watch. "That's a lot of gold for a lad to be carrying. May I see it?" While the captain examined the watch, Peter explained about Grandfather and the gifts. The captain said, "Well, I was going to offer to buy your watch, but I can see it means more to you than money."

Later, on the train from New York to Missouri, the conductor noticed the watch chained through Peter's vest pocket and wanted to know how he got such a valuable timepiece. Once again Peter explained about Grandfather's gifts and the questions,

What have you done with your name?
What have you done with your time?

"That's a keeper, lad," said the conductor. "Don't lose that watch, and don't sell it. Just mind it."

The train journey ended at the Missouri River. From there, the only way to get to the Valley of the Great Salt Lake in Utah Territory was on foot or horseback, by wagon or handcart. At the station where Peter's family outfitted a covered wagon and a team of oxen, a teamster called to Peter, "How much you want for that fancy gold watch, eh boy? You want to trade it for a pony to cross the plains? Or how about a little wager for the watch?" He laughed and took dice out of his pocket. Peter ducked around a wagon and didn't answer. The next morning he and his family were rolling westward in a covered wagon.

The ocean had seemed like endless water to Peter, but the prairie was a sea of grasses that felt endless, too. The seasickness was gone, but other sickness was worse. Peter's father became ill after leaving the outfitting post at the Missouri River, and each day his fever worsened. Peter tried to help his mother and comfort his sisters. In the daytime, he took his father's turn driving the wagon. At night, he sat by his father's side and talked about what life had been like in Denmark and what it might be like in Utah Territory.

But Peter's father did not get better. He ached and moaned with the sickness they couldn't name. To comfort him, Peter slipped the watch under his father's ear. "It will feel cool against your fever, and the ticking will remind you to keep ticking yourself." Peter tried to make his father smile, but nothing seemed to help.

Somewhere in Nebraska Territory, far away from their old home in Denmark and still a long way from their new home in Utah Territory, Peter's father died.

Peter had seen people buried at sea. He had seen them buried on the prairie. But he had never thought his own father would be one of them. He helped dig the grave in the hard, tough sod. The wagon company gathered with Peter's grieving mother and family for words of last good-bye, and then they moved on.

Peter rubbed the gold watch and tried to hold back tears. The excitement and sense of adventure he had felt about the journey were gone. Everything was becoming more difficult. Food was running low, and shoes were wearing out. Oxen were going lame, and wagon wheels were breaking. Peter missed his father, and for the first time he wished to be back in Denmark with Grandfather.

Peter's family shared their wagon with a man named Mr. Tereson. He had paid for half the wagon and team even though he had no family of his own. After Peter's father died, Mr. Tereson began to talk about going back. He said the journey was getting too hard, and it wasn't worth getting killed by Indians or starving in the mountains. Peter and his mother refused to give up or turn back. They were determined to go on, even though Mr. Tereson kept grumbling and threatening.

One day it was their turn to bring up the rear in the wagon train. Hidden by the dust of the long line of prairie schooners, Mr. Tereson slowed the oxen until they were far behind. Then he dumped the family's belongings on the ground, turned the wagon around, and headed back east. Peter clung to the wagon, shouting, "Don't go! Please don't leave us here!" Peter felt the watch nudging against his pocket, and suddenly he had an idea that might save them.

"Stay!" he bargained frantically. "Stay, and I'll give you Grandfather's gold watch!"

"No!" Mr. Tereson shouted. "I wouldn't stay for a trunkful of gold watches."

No amount of pleading could stop Mr. Tereson, and soon the fatherless family was alone on the vast prairie.

Peter helped his mother and sisters gather their things and build a small camp for the night. In the morning they would try to figure out what to do. That night Peter had trouble falling asleep. He fingered the watch for a long time and tried not to think about wolves and snakes and Indians and what might be out there in the dark.

The next day the leader of the wagon company rode back to find them. A rescue wagon was sent, and within three days they caught up with the group. Because Peter's family no longer had a wagon of their own, they were assigned to travel with other families.

Peter was asked to help Widow Sorenson pull her handcart. When he pushed his chest against the heavy wooden bar of the handcart, it pressed against the watch. Peter was afraid he had damaged the watch and quickly pulled it from his vest pocket. It was still ticking. He smiled and polished the watch on his shirtsleeve. Then he dropped it into a deep pocket in his threadbare pants.

"That's a fine treasure you have there," said Widow Sorenson. "I had treasures, too. My husband and three children were treasure enough, but they are all gone now. One by one they died of the fever." She turned her sunbonnet-shaded face to look Peter in the eyes. "I can't make it over the mountains without help. I'm tired and alone. Thank you for helping me. Your heart's as good as gold, lad—as good as the gold in that fine watch."

As they pushed and pulled the handcart through the mountains, Peter told Widow Sorenson the story of Grandfather and the gold watch and the questions,

What have you done with your name?

What have you done with your time?

On their last evening before arriving in the Valley of the Great Salt Lake, the travelers felt excitement and relief. Singing and a better-than-usual supper made everyone feel good. Peter ate campfire biscuits and bean stew, and for once his stomach felt full. He rubbed his skinny belly and reached in his pocket for the watch. He froze with disbelief. It was gone! The pocket was empty! He pulled the pocket inside out and stared at a frayed hole. "It can't be gone," he moaned. "It can't be. I must find it. Where, oh where?" He searched all around the campfire and the wagons, but it was nowhere to be found.

Peter went to bed heartsick. In the morning everyone looked for the watch while they broke camp, but it was still missing when the command came to move on. As the wagon train lumbered out of the mountains into the Valley, the people were both happy and sad. They were happy the journey was over, yet sad because many had lost much more than a gold watch.

At the settlement in the Salt Lake Valley, people turned out to greet and help the new arrivals. This was the place! With their travels over ocean and plains ended, Peter and his family settled into a new way of life. There was much hard work ahead.

Peter helped build his mother's house. He planted a garden, herded sheep, and started an orchard. As he worked, he often thought of Grandfather and his words. The orchard grew, and so did Peter. With time, he became a respected farmer. Eventually he married, had a fine family, and became the mayor of a little town near Salt Lake City. He became known as a good speaker and storyteller. Many of his stories were about leaving Denmark and crossing the ocean and plains as a boy. Sometimes he told the story about the lost gold watch and Grandfather's questions,

What have you done with your name?
What have you done with your time?

Forty years after Peter crossed the plains, Utah Territory became the forty-fifth state in the United States of America. The year was 1896, and Peter was one of the speakers at the statehood celebration in Salt Lake City. There were flags and decorations and bands and music and speeches. Peter's speech was about the pioneers who had made the desert blossom like a rose. When it was over, a man in the audience shook Peter's hand.

"So, you are Peter Nels Jorgensen," he said. "Fine speech you gave. Had you not been a speaker at the celebration today I might never have found you. I have known your name for forty years, but I never expected to find you." With a smile he took a gold watch from his vest pocket and opened the watchcase. The name inscribed on it was just as clear as it had been the day Grandfather gave it to Peter over forty years ago.

"Where did you get this watch?" Peter asked in amazement. "My grandfather gave it to me in Denmark. I lost it as a boy on my way to Utah."

The man said, "Many years ago, I also crossed the plains with a wagon company. I was headed for California to find gold and strike it rich. Your watch was the most gold I ever found. It was glinting in the sunlight under a sagebrush as I passed by."

That evening Peter sat in the rocking chair on his front porch and marveled at the watch that had come back to him. He caressed the watch and turned it over and over the way he had done as a boy. He opened the watchcase and looked at the name he and Grandfather shared. "Now I am the grandfather," said Peter with a quiet chuckle.

He sat and thought quietly for a long time. Then he called to his grandson who was sitting on the porch steps whittling a new whistle with his pocketknife.

"Nels, my boy, how old are you?"

"Twelve next week" was the answer.

Peter sat down on the steps by the boy. Carefully he placed the gold watch in the hand of his surprised grandson. He folded the young fingers over the treasure with his own worn fingers. "Nels, this is a gift from your grandfather and your great-great-grandfather. It is much more than just a birthday present, you know." Peter smiled. "Someday you will pass it on. In the meantime, take good care of it, and imagine the stories it would tell if it could talk. When you hear it ticking, you must always remember to ask yourself,

What have I done with my name?

What have I done with my time?

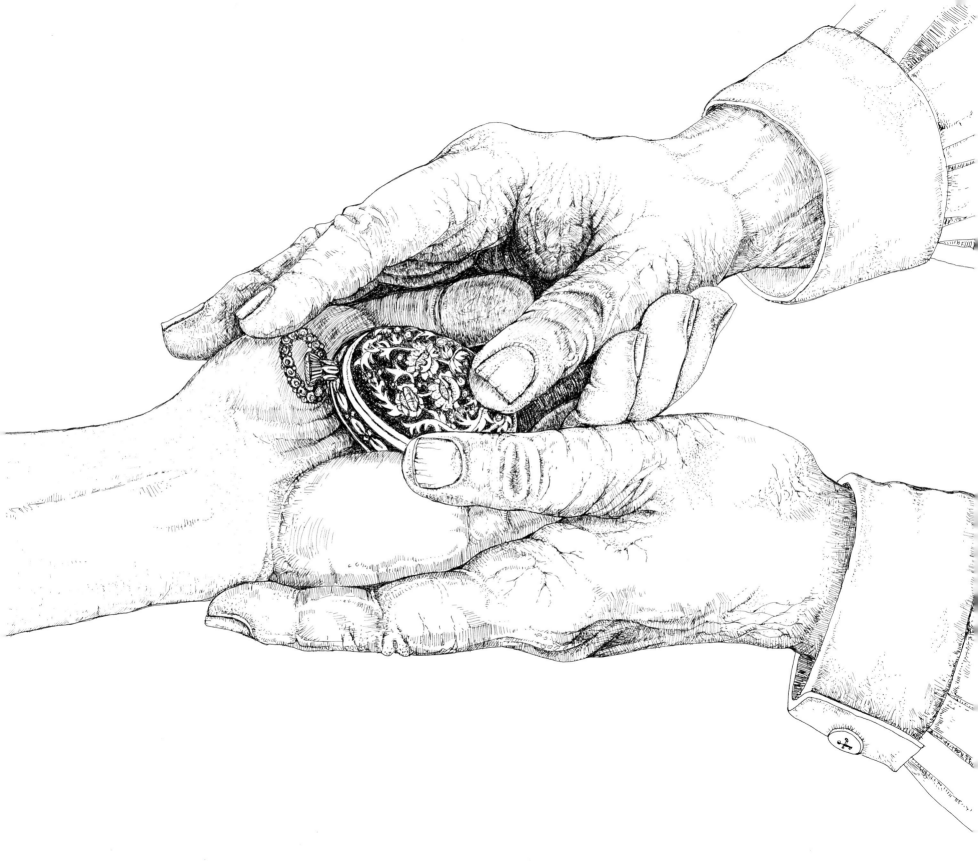

That night, long after Grandfather Peter had gone into the house, Nels sat quietly on the porch fingering the gold watch and thinking,

What will I do with my name?

What will I do with my time?